Earth & Ashes

Earth & Ashes

ATIQ RAHIMI

Translated from Dari (Afghanistan) by
Erdağ M. Göknar

Chatto & Windus · London

Published by Chatto & Windus 2002

2 4 6 8 10 9 7 5 3 1

Copyright © P.O.L éditeur, 2000
Translation copyright © Erdağ M. Göknar, 2002
First published in Dari (Afghanistan) in 1999
by Éditions Khavaran, France,
under the title *Khâkestar-o-khâk*

First published in Great Britain in 2002 by
Chatto & Windus
Random House, 20 Vauxhall Bridge Road,
London SW1V 2SA

Random House Australia (Pty) Limited
20 Alfred Street, Milsons Point, Sydney,
New South Wales 2061, Australia

Random House New Zealand Limited
18 Poland Road, Glenfield,
Auckland 10, New Zealand

Random House South Africa (Pty) Limited
Endulini, 5A Jubilee Road, Parktown 2193, South Africa

The Random House Group Limited Reg. No. 954009

A CIP catalogue record for this book
is available from the British Library

ISBN 0701173750

Papers used by Random House are natural,
recyclable products made from wood grown in sustainable forests.
The manufacturing processes conform to the environmental
regulations of the country of origin

Typeset by Deltatype Ltd, Birkenhead, Merseyside
Printed and bound in Great Britain by
Biddles Ltd, Guilford and King's Lynn

For my father, and other fathers
who wept during the war

The author and publisher would like to thank
Sabrina Nouri for her editorial advice.

A Note on the Text

Reference is made in *Earth and Ashes* to the great eleventh-century Persian epic, the *Book of Kings* (*Shahnama* in Persian) by Ferdusi. This famous poem interweaves Persian myths, legends and historical events to tell the history of Iran and its neighbours from the creation of the world to the Arab conquest in the seventh century. Even today, storytellers can recount large parts of the *Book of Kings* from memory. The characters mentioned in *Earth and Ashes* are:

ROSTAM, son of Zal, the great hero of the epic who, in a battle, kills his son, Sohrab, whose existence he did not know about.

SOHRAB, son of Rostam, born from Rostam's secret union with Tahmina, daughter of the King of Samengan, who finds himself on the opposite side from his father in battle and is killed by him.

ZOHAK, the legendary tyrant of the epic, who ruled with serpents who fed off the brains of the young men in his kingdom.

He has a great heart,
as great as his sorrow

Rafaat Hosseini

'I'm hungry.'

You take an apple from the scarf you've tied into a bundle and wipe it on your dusty clothes. The apple just gets dirtier. You put it back in the bundle and pull out another, cleaner one, which you give to your grandson, Yassin, who is sitting next to you, his head resting on your tired arm. The child takes it in his small, dirty hands and brings it to his mouth. His front teeth haven't come through yet. He tries to bite with his canines. His hollow, chapped cheeks twitch. His narrow eyes become narrower. The apple is sour. He wrinkles up his small nose and gasps.

With your back to the autumn sun, you are squatting against the iron railings of the bridge that links the two banks of the dry riverbed north of Pul-i-Khumri. The road connecting Northern Afghanistan to Kabul passes over this very bridge. If you turn left on the far side of the bridge, on to the dirt track that winds between the scrub-covered hills, you arrive at the Karkar coal mine . . .

The sound of Yassin whimpering tears your thoughts away from the mine. Look, your grandson can't bite the apple. Where's that knife? You search your pockets and find it. Taking the apple from his hands, you cut it in half, then in half again and hand the pieces back to him. You put the knife in a pocket and fold your arms over your chest.

You haven't had any naswar for a while. Where's the tin? You search your pockets again. Eventually you find it and put a pinch of naswar in your mouth. Before returning the tin to your pocket, you glance at your reflection in its mirrored lid. Your narrow eyes are set deep in their sockets. Time has left its mark on the surrounding skin, a web of sinuous lines like thirsty worms waiting round a hole. The turban on your head is unravelling. Its weight forces your head into your shoulders. It is covered in dust. Maybe it's the dust that makes it so heavy. Its original colour is no longer apparent. The sun and the dust have turned it grey . . .

Put the box back. Think of something else. Look at something else.

You put the tin back into one of your pockets. You draw your hand over your grey-streaked beard, then clasp your knees and stare at your tired shadow which merges with the orderly shadows cast by the railings of the bridge.

An army truck, a red star on its door, passes over the bridge. It disturbs the stony sleep of the dry earth. The dust rises. It engulfs the bridge then settles. Silently it covers everything, dusting the apples, your turban, your eyelids . . . You put your hand over Yassin's apple to shield it.

'Don't!' your grandson shouts. Your hand prevents him from eating.

'You want to eat dust, child?'

'Don't!'

Leave him alone. Keep yourself to yourself. The dust fills your mouth and nostrils. You spit your naswar out next to five other small green plugs on the ground. With the loose flap of your turban, you cover your nose and mouth. You look over at the mouth of the bridge, at the road to the mine. At the black wooden hut of the guard posted at the road barrier. Wisps of smoke fly from its little window. After hesitating for several seconds you grip hold of one of the bridge's rusty railings with one hand and grab your bundle with the other. Pulling yourself to your feet, you shuffle in the direction of the hut. Yassin gets up too and follows you, clinging to your clothes. Together you approach the hut. You put your head through the small, paneless window. The hut is full of smoke and there's the smell of coal. The guard is in exactly the same position as he was before, his back against one of the walls, his eyes still closed. His cap might have been pulled slightly further down, but that's all. Everything else is just the same, even the half-smoked cigarette between his dry lips . . .

Try coughing.

Even you can't hear your cough, let alone the guard. Cough again, a bit louder. He doesn't hear that either. Let's hope the smoke hasn't suffocated him. You call out.

'Brother . . .'

'What do you want now, old man?'

He can speak, thank goodness. He's alive. But he's still motionless, his eyes closed under his cap . . . Your tongue moves, preparing to say something. Don't interrupt him!

'. . . You're killing me. I told you a hundred times. When a car comes past, I'll throw myself in its path, I'll beg them to take you to the mine. What else do you want? Till now have you seen any cars? No? You want someone else's word?'

'I wouldn't dream of it, my good brother. I know there's been no car. But you never know . . . What if you were to forget us . . .'

'How on earth do you expect me to forget, old man? If you want I can recite your life story. You told it to me enough times. Your son works at the mine, you are here with his son to see him.'

'My God, you remember everything . . . It's me who's losing my memory. I thought I hadn't told you. Sometimes I think others forget the way I do. I'm sorry. I've bothered you . . .'

The truth is, your heart is burdened. It's been a long time since a friend or even a stranger listened to you. A long time since a friend or stranger warmed your heart with their words. You want to talk and to listen. Go on, speak to him! But you're unlikely to get a response. The guard won't listen to you. He is deep in his own thoughts. Preoccupied with himself. Let him be.

You stand silently in front of the hut, gazing away from it at the pitch and roll of the valley. The valley is dried out, covered in thorn bushes

– silent. And at the end of the valley is Murad, your son.

You turn away from the valley and stare back inside the hut. You want to tell the guard that you're only waiting here like this for a vehicle to pass because of your grandson Yassin. If you were alone, you'd have set out on foot a long time ago. For you, walking four or five hours is nothing. Each and every day you're on your feet working for ten hours, or longer, working your land. You're a courageous man . . . So what? Why tell the guard all this? What's it to him? Nothing. Then let him be. Sleep in peace, brother . . . We're off. We won't bother you again.

But you don't go. You stand there quietly.

The click of colliding stones at your feet draws your attention to Yassin. He is squatting down, crushing a piece of apple between two stones.
'What are you doing? For God's sake! Eat your apple!'
You grab Yassin by the shoulders and pull him to his feet. The child shouts:
'Don't! Let me go . . . Why don't these stones make any noise?'
The smell of smoke escaping from the hut mingles with the roar of the guard's voice:
'You're killing me! Can't you keep your grandson quiet for one minute?'
You don't have the chance to apologize, or rather, you can't face it. You take hold of

5

Yassin's hand and drag him to the bridge. You drop back down to the ground against the iron railings, put the bundle by your side and, wrapping your arms around the little boy, scold him:

'Will you behave!'

To whom are you speaking? To Yassin? He can't even hear the sound of stones, let alone your feeble voice. Yassin's world is now another world, one of silence. He wasn't deaf. He became deaf. He doesn't realise this. He's surprised that nothing makes a sound anymore. Until a few days ago it wasn't this way.

Just imagine. You're a child, Yassin, who heard perfectly well just a short time ago, a child who didn't even know what 'deafness' was. And then, one day, suddenly you can't hear a sound. Why? It would be idiotic to try and tell you it was deafness. You don't hear, you don't understand. You don't think it's you who can't hear; you think others have become mute. People have lost their voices; stones have lost their sound. The world is silent . . . So then, why are people moving their mouths?

Yassin hides his small, question-filled face under your clothes.

Your gaze is drawn over the side of the bridge, to the dried-up river that has become a bed of black stones and scrub. You look above the riverbed to the rocky mountains in the distance. They merge with Murad's face.

'Why have you come, Father? Is everything all right?' he asks.

For more than a week now, this face with this question has haunted your days and your nights.

Why have you come? The question gnaws at your bones. Can't that brain in your head find an answer? If only there were no such question. No such word as 'why'. You've come to see how your son's doing. That's all. After all, you're a father, you think about your son from time to time. Is it a sin? No. You know why you've really come.

You look for your box of naswar, tip a little into the palm of your hand, and put it under your tongue. If only things were simple, full of pleasure – like naswar, like sleep . . . Your gaze rises above the summits of the mountains to the sky . . . But Murad's face still mingles with the mountains. The rocks are slowly becoming hot; they're turning red. It is as if they have become coal and the mountains are one great furnace. The coal catches fire, erupting from the mountain and flowing down the dry riverbed towards you. You are on one side of the river, Murad is on the other. Murad keeps asking, 'Why have you come? Why have you come alone with Yassin? Why have you given Yassin silent stones?'

Then Murad starts to cross over to you.

'Murad,' you shout, 'stay where you are, child! It's a river of fire. You'll get burned! Don't come!'

You ask yourself who could believe such a thing: a river of flowing fire? Have you become a seer of visions? Look, Murad's wading through the river without getting burned. No, he must be getting burned, but he's not reacting. Murad is strong. He doesn't break down. Look at him. His body is covered in sweat.

'Murad,' you shout again, 'Stop! The river's on fire!'

But Murad continues to move towards you, asking, 'Why have you come? Why have you come?'

From somewhere, you're not sure where, the voice of Murad's mother rises.

'Dastaguir, tell him to stay there. *You* cross the river. Take my apple-blossom patterned scarf with you and go and wipe away his sweat. Take my scarf for Murad . . .'

Your eyes open. You feel your skin covered in cold sweat. You're not able to sleep in peace. It's been a week now since you've had a restful sleep. As soon as you close your eyes, it's Murad and his mother or Yassin and his mother or fire and ash or shouts and wails . . . and you wake up again. Your eyes burn. They burn with sleeplessness. Your eyes don't see anymore. They're exhausted. Out of exhaustion and sleeplessness you keep falling into a half-sleep – a half-sleep filled with visions. It's as if you live only in these images and dreams. Images and dreams of what you've witnessed and wish you hadn't . . . maybe also what you yet must see, wishing you didn't have to.

If only you slept like a child, like Yassin. Yassin?

No, like any other child but Yassin, who whimpers and moans in his sleep. Maybe Yassin's sleep has become like yours, full of images, dirt, fire, screams, and tears . . . No, not like Yassin's. Like any other child's. Like a baby's. A sleep without images, memories – without dreams.

If only it were possible to begin life again from the beginning, like a newborn baby. You'd like to live again, if only for a day, an hour, a minute, a second.

You think for a moment about the time Murad left the village, when he walked out through the door. You too should have left the village with your wife and children and your grandchildren and gone to another village. You should've gone to Pul-i-Khumri. Never mind if you'd had no land, no crops, no work. May the land rot in Hell! You would have followed Murad. You would have worked in the mines, shoulder-to-shoulder with him. Then today, no one would be asking you why you've come.

If only . . .

Over the four years Murad has worked at the mine, you haven't had a single chance to visit him. It's been four years since he entrusted his young wife and his son Yassin to you and left for the mine to earn his living.

The truth is, Murad wanted to flee the village

9

and its inhabitants. He wanted to go far away.
So he left . . . Thank God he left.

Four years ago your neighbour Yaqub Shah's
unworthy son made advances towards Murad's
wife, and your daughter-in-law told Murad.
Grabbing a spade, Murad ran to Yaqub Shah's
house, demanded his son come out and, without asking questions or waiting for answers,
brought the spade hard down on to the crown of
his head. Yaqub Shah took his wounded son to
the village council, and Murad was sentenced
to six months in prison.

After he was freed, Murad collected his things
together and left for the mine. Since then he has
only returned to the village four times. It hasn't
even been a month since his last visit and now
you're going to the mine to see him, holding his
son by the hand. He'll definitely wonder why.

'Water!'

With Yassin's shout, your eyes drop from the
mountains to the dry riverbed, and from the
riverbed to the parched lips of your grandson.
'From where should I get water, child?'
You glance furtively towards the guard's
wooden hut. You don't have the nerve to ask
him for water again. This morning you took
some from his jug for Yassin, and if you ask him
again . . . No, this time he'll get angry and bring
the jug down on your head . . . Better ask
elsewhere.
Shading your eyes with your hand, you scan

the other end of the bridge. This morning you stopped at a little makeshift shop there to ask the shopkeeper the way to the mine, and the man was kind. Go there again and ask him for water. You start to rise, but then remain nailed to the ground. If a vehicle goes past and the guard doesn't see you, all this waiting will have been for nothing. No, you'd better stay put. The guard isn't the sort of man to wait for you, or call out to you ... No, Dastaguir, stay just where you are.

'Water, Grandfather, water!'

Yassin is sobbing. You kneel down, take an apple from your bundle and hold it out to him.

'No, I want water, water!'

You let the apple drop to the ground, heave yourself up, grab Yassin with one hand and the bundle with the other, and hurry off towards the shop.

The shop is just a small wooden stand with three mud walls. At the front, four uneven planks form a window that is covered with plastic sheeting. Behind a small opening sits a black-bearded man. His shaven head is hidden by an embroidered cap and he wears a black waistcoat. A large pair of scales almost completely obscures his thin torso. He is bent over a book. At the sound of your footsteps, he raises his head and adjusts his spectacles on his nose. Despite his pensive expression, his eyes, magnified by the thick lenses, are strikingly bright.

He greets you with a kind smile and asks, 'Back
from the mine?'

You spit your naswar on to the ground and
respond meekly.

'No, my good brother, we haven't gone to the
mine yet. We're waiting for a vehicle to pass.
My grandson is very thirsty. Would you be kind
enough to give him a little water . . .'

The shopkeeper pours some water from his
jug into a copper cup. On the back wall of the
shop there's a large painting: behind a large
rock, a man holds the Devil fast by the arm.
Both of them are watching an old man who has
fallen into a deep pit.

The shopkeeper hands the cup to Yassin and
asks, 'Have you come far?'

'From Abqul. My son works in the mine. I am
going to see him.'

You keep your eye on the guard's hut.

'It was a bad state of affairs over there, wasn't
it?'

The shopkeeper tries to begin a conversation
but you keep your eyes fixed on the hut. You
remain silent, as if you haven't heard anything.
If you are honest, you did not want to hear. Or
rather, you don't want to answer. Come on,
brother, let Dastaguir be!

'I hear the Russians reduced the whole village
to smoke and ashes last week. Is it true?'

You'll have no peace. You came for water, not
tears. A mouthful of water, nothing more.

Brother, by the grace of God, don't pour salt on our wounds.

What is this, Dastaguir? Moments ago your heart was heavy. You wanted to talk to anyone about anything. Now, here is someone who'll listen to what lies in your heart, whose look alone is a comfort. Say something!
Without taking your eyes off the hut, you answer, 'Yes, brother. I was there. I saw everything. I saw my own death . . .'

You fall silent. If you get involved in a conversation, you might forget about the vehicle.

The shopkeeper takes off his glasses and pokes his head out the window to see what interests you so much. As soon as he sees the hut, he understands. He sits back behind his large pair of scales.
'My good brother, it's still too early. A vehicle always comes by around two. You've got two hours ahead of you.'
'At two? Why didn't the guard say anything?'
'Probably because he isn't too sure himself. It's not his fault. The cars and lorries come at odd times. Besides, what's on time in this country that transport should be? These days . . .'
'Grandfather, jujube fruits!'
Yassin's words interrupt the shopkeeper. You take the copper cup from Yassin's hands. He hasn't finished it.
'First drink your water.'

'I want jujubes, jujubes!'

You put the cup to Yassin's mouth and gesture impatiently for him to finish. Yassin turns his head away and continues in a voice choked with sobs, 'Jujubes! Jujubes!'

The shopkeeper reaches out through the shop window and passes Yassin a handful of fruit. The child grabs it and sits down at your feet. And you, cup of water in hand, try to keep your temper. God help me. You sigh.

'That child will make a madman of me.'

'Don't say that, father. He's a child. He doesn't understand.'

You sigh again, more deeply than before and say, 'I'm afraid, brother, the problem isn't that he can't understand . . . The child has gone deaf.'

'May God heal him! What happened?'

You finish the remainder of your grandson's water and continue, 'He lost his hearing during the bombing of the village. I don't know how to make him understand. I speak to him the same as before. I still scold him . . . It's just habit . . .'

As you talk, you pass the copper cup back through the window. The man takes it and looks sympathetically at Yassin, then at you, then at the empty cup . . . He prefers silence. Like a ghost, he withdraws into the shop. His hand reaches for a small bowl on one of the wooden shelves. He fills it with tea and hands it to you.

'Take a mouthful of tea, good brother. You're exhausted. You still have plenty of time. I know all the vehicles that go to the mine. If one comes, I'll tell you.'

You glance over at the guard's hut and, after a moment's hesitation, take the bowl of tea, saying, 'You're a man with a good heart. May your forbears rest in peace!'

The sound of your sipping brings a kind smile to the shopkeeper's lips.

'If you're feeling cold, come inside; your grandson also looks cold.'

'God bless you, brother, it's fine here. There's sun. We don't want to disturb you any more. What if a car were to come. I'll drink my tea and we'll be gone.'

'Father, I just told you. I'll let you know if a car comes. You can see them pass from here. Now, if you don't want to stay, that's another story.'

'I swear to you, brother, it's not a matter of wanting or not wanting. That guard isn't the kind of man to make a car wait.'

'Dear father, it takes a long time for him to issue a pass and then open the barrier. And he isn't a bad man, that guard. I know him. He comes here a lot. It's sorrow that has ruined him.'

The man falls silent. He puts a cigarette into the corner of his mouth and lights it. Then he goes on:

'You know, father, sorrow can turn to water and spill from your eyes, or it can sharpen your tongue into a sword, or it can become a time bomb that, one day, will explode and destroy you . . . The sorrow of Fateh the guard is like all three. When he comes to see me, his sadness flows out in tears. If he remains alone in his hut, it becomes a bomb . . . When he steps out of the hut and sees others, his sorrow turns itself into a sword and he wants to . . .'

You don't hear the rest of the shopkeeper's words. Your thoughts pull you inwards, to where your own misery lies. Which has your sorrow become? Tears? No, otherwise you'd cry. A sword? No, you haven't wounded anyone yet. A bomb? You're still living. You can't describe your sorrow; it hasn't taken shape yet. It hasn't had a chance to show itself. If only it wouldn't take shape at all. If only it would fall silent, be forgotten . . . It will be so, of course it will . . . As soon as you see Murad, your son . . . Where are you Murad?

'Good father, where have you drifted off to?'
   The shopkeeper's question brings you back from your interior journey. You reply humbly.
   'Nothing, brother, you were talking of sorrow . . .'

You finish the tea in one gulp and give the empty bowl back to the shopkeeper. You pat your pockets, take out your box of naswar and put a pinch into your mouth. Then you go and sit at the base of one of the wooden posts propping up the shop's corrugated-iron roof. Yassin plays silently with the stones from the

jujube fruit. You take him by the arm and pull
him to your side. You want to say something
but the sound of footsteps silences you. A man
in military uniform approaches.

'*Salaam*, Mirza Qadir.'

'*Waleykom Salaam*, Hashmet Khan.'

The soldier asks for a pack of cigarettes and
engages Mirza Qadir in conversation.

At your feet, your grandson is busy playing with
an ant attracted by the naswar you have spat
out on to the ground. Yassin mixes the naswar,
the earth and the ant together with a jujube
stone. The insect squirms in the green mud.

The soldier says goodbye to Mirza Qadir, and
walks past you.

Yassin digs with his jujube stone at a foot-
print left by the soldier.

The ant is no longer there. Ant, mud and
naswar are stuck to the boot of the departing
soldier.

Mirza Qadir abandons his spot behind the
scales and withdraws to a corner of the shop to
perform his midday prayers.

It has been a week now since you've been to the
mosque or prayed. So, have you forgotten about
God? No, your clothes are not in a fit state for
prayer. This same pair of clothes has been on
your back day and night for a week. Yet, God is
merciful . . .

Whether you pray or not, the reality is that
God isn't concerned with you. If only he'd turn

his attention to you for a moment, if only he'd come to your side . . . No, God has forsaken his subjects. If this is how he looks after his subjects, you yourself, in your absolute ruin, could be lord of a thousand worlds!

God help me! Dastaguir you're committing blasphemy. Damn the temptations of Satan. Damn you.

Occupy your thoughts with something else. But what?

Aren't you hungry? Spit out your naswar.

'My good man, your tongue will wear out. Your insides will wear out. For days naswar has been your bread and water.'

You hear the words Murad's mother would say to you before you sat down to eat. When Murad was in prison, you would make up excuses to avoid coming to the table. Naswar under your tongue, you'd disappear into the little garden saying that you wanted to catch the last rays of daylight or that you had weeding to do. You would sit among the plants, and open your laden heart to the earth and flowers. Your wife's voice would boom out into the courtyard declaring that, after your death until the Day of Judgement, your mouth would fill with earth and your body would turn to earth from which a tobacco field would grow. In Hell you would burn in an inferno of tobacco leaves . . . for ever.

You have yet to face Judgement Day and you are already burning. Who needs the flames of Hell and a bonfire of tobacco?

You spit out your naswar. You take a piece of

bread out of the bundle and share it with
Yassin.

Your teeth aren't able to chew the bread. No,
they are. It's the bread that is at fault. It is days
old and hard. If there's one thing that's still all
right, it's your teeth. You have teeth, but no
bread. If only you had the right to choose: teeth
or bread. Would that be free will?

You take an apple from the bag and recom-
mence your conversation with God. You
request that He lower himself from the
heavens. You untie and spread out the apple-
blossom scarf as if to invite him to share your
dry bread. You want to ask him what it is you
have done to deserve such a destiny.

'The soldier says the Russians destroyed the
village.'

Mirza Qadir comes between you and God.
You bless him for asking you a question that
prevents you from continuing your argument
with God. You ask for divine mercy and
respond to Mirza Qadir.

'Don't ask, brother. They didn't spare a single
life . . . I don't understand why God saw fit to
punish us . . . The village was reduced to dust.'

'Why did they attack?'

'My friend, in this country, if you wonder
why something happened, you have to start by
making the dead talk. What do we understand?
A while back a group of government trouble-
makers came to our village to enlist fighters for
the Russians. Half the young people fled, the

other half hid. On the pretext of searching the houses, the government soldiers wrecked and looted everything. In the middle of the night, men from the next village arrived and killed the government soldiers . . . The next morning they left with the men who had hidden to avoid serving under the red flag . . . Not even a day had passed before the Russians came and surrounded the village. I was at the mill. Suddenly, there was an explosion. I ran out. I saw fire and clouds of dust. I ran in the direction of my house. Why wasn't I killed before I reached home? What wrong had I committed to be condemned to witness . . .'

Your throat is seized with sobs. Tears well in your eyes. No, they are not tears. Your grief is melting and overflowing. Let it flow!

Mirza Qadir, stunned into silence in the entrance of his shop, looks like a portrait; as if he has become part of the scene on the wall behind him.

'I ran towards the house through the dust and fire. Before I arrived, I saw Yassin's mother. She was running, completely naked . . . She wasn't shouting, she was laughing. She was running about like a madwoman. She had been in the bathhouse. A bomb had hit and destroyed it. Women were buried alive and died. But my daughter-in-law . . . If only I'd been blind and hadn't seen her dishonoured. I ran after her. She vanished into the smoke and flames. I came to the house, not knowing how I'd found it. There was nothing left . . . The house had become a grave. A grave for my wife, a grave for my other son, his wife and their children . . .'

A sob constricts your throat. A tear drops from your eye. With the loose flap of your turban, you wipe it away:

'Only my grandson survived. But he doesn't understand what I say. I feel like I'm speaking to a stone. It tears me to pieces . . . It's not enough to talk, brother. If your words aren't heard, those words turn to tears . . .'

You hug Yassin's head against your body. The child raises his eyes and looks at you. He stands and calls out, 'Grandfather's crying. My uncle's dead, Mummy's gone . . . Qader's dead, Grand-ma's dead!'

Each time Yassin sees you crying, he repeats these words. Each time, he goes on to describe the bombing, miming it with his hands:

'The bomb was huge. It brought silence. The tanks took away people's voices and left. They even took Grandfather's voice away. Grandfather can't talk anymore, he can't tell me off . . .'

The child laughs and runs towards the guard's hut.

You call to him. 'Come back! Where are you going?'

It's useless. Let him play.

Mirza Qadir, who has been silent till now, as if unable to find words to lessen your suffering, mumbles something under his breath and offers you his condolences. Then he starts to speak, in a calm, measured way:

'Venerable father, these days the dead are more fortunate than the living. What are we to do? We're on the eve of destruction. Men have lost all sense of honour. Power has become their faith instead of faith being their power. There are no longer any courageous men. Who now remembers the story of the hero Rostam? Today, it is Sohrab, his son, who murders his very own father and, excuse the expression, screws his own mother. We are once again at the mercy of the tyrant Zohak's snakes – snakes which feed on the minds of the young . . .'

He breaks off to light a cigarette, points to the scene painted on the wall and adds, 'Actually, it is today's youth who are Zohaks. They're on the same path as the Devil, pushing their own fathers into a pit . . . and one day soon their own snakes will devour their minds.'

He gazes into your eyes. Your eyes are fixed on the entrance to the shop. The interior has become a spacious room at the far end of which your uncle sits by his water pipe. You are a child of about Yassin's age. You sit at your uncle's feet as he recites Ferdusi's epic, the *Book of Kings*. He speaks of Rostam; of Sohrab; of Tahmina . . . He tells of the battle between father and son, of the talisman that saved Rostam, of the death of Sohrab . . . Your younger brother starts crying and rushes from the room to go and lay his head on your mother's lap.

'No, Sohrab is stronger than Rostam!' he sobs.

Your mother says, 'Yes, my child, Sohrab *is* stronger than Rostam.'

And you cry, too, but you don't leave the room. In silence, with tear-filled eyes, you remain at your uncle's feet, waiting to know whether Rostam will go on fighting after Sohrab's death . . .

Mirza Qadir's cough brings you back from your childhood.

The shop returns to being small. Mirza Qadir's head appears in the window frame.

'Are you going to the mine to work with your son?'

'No, brother, I've come only to see him . . . He knows nothing of the misfortune that has struck the family. On the one hand there's the misery of the bombing, on the other, the misery of telling such a thing to my own son. How should I tell him? I don't know. He's not the type to take it quietly . . . You'd be able to take his life before you offended his honour. He has a temper . . .'

You bring your hand to your forehead and close your eyes.

'My son, my only son will surely go mad. It would be better if I didn't tell him.'

'He's strong, father. You must tell him. He must accept it. One day or another he'll find out. It is better that he hear it from you, that you tell him you are with him and share the burden of his sorrow. Don't leave him alone. Make him understand that man's fate contains such things, that he is not alone, that he has both you and his son, that you are his source of strength and that he is yours. These hardships are everyone's fate, war has no mercy . . .'

Mirza Qadir moves closer and lowers his voice.

'The law of war is the law of the sacrifice. In sacrifice, there is either blood on your throat or on your hands.'

'Why?' you ask naively.

Mirza Qadir tosses his cigarette butt away. In the same soft tone, he adds, 'Brother, the logic of war is the logic of sacrifice. There's no 'why' about it. What matters is the act alone, not the cause or the effect.'

He falls silent. He reads your eyes for the impact of his words. You nod your head as if you have understood. You wonder what the logic of war could possibly be. His words in themselves are well and good, but they're no cure for the troubles you and your son share. Murad is not a man who listens to advice or thinks about the law or logic of war. To him, blood is the only answer for blood. He'll take vengeance, even at the cost of his own neck. That's all there is to it. And he won't care too much if he has blood on his hands either.

'Old man, where are you? Come before your grandson drives me mad!'

The guard's shouts alarm you. You jump up,

shouting, 'Here I am, I'm coming!' as you run back to the hut.

Yassin is standing in front of the hut, tossing stones at it. The guard has taken shelter and is roaring with fury. You reach Yassin, slap him smartly on his small head and take the stones out of his hands. The furious guard emerges.

'Your grandson's gone mad. He began throwing stones at the hut. It didn't matter what I said to him, he didn't pay a blind bit of notice . . .'

'I'm sorry, brother. The child is deaf. He can't hear a word . . .'

You take Yassin back towards the shop. Mirza Qadir comes out and makes his way towards the guard, laughing. You take up your place against the wooden post again and hug Yassin's head to your chest.

Yassin doesn't cry. As usual, he's bewildered.

'Have tanks come here, too?' he asks.

'How should I know? Be quiet!'

You both fall silent. You both know that questions and answers are in vain. But then Yassin continues:

'They must've come and taken the voice of the shopkeeper and the voice of the guard . . . Grandfather, have the Russians come and taken away everyone's voice? What do they do with all the voices? Why did you let them take away your voice? If you hadn't, would they've killed you? Grandma didn't give them her voice and she's dead. If she were here she'd tell me the story of Baba Kharkash . . . No, if she were here, she'd have no voice . . .'

He falls silent for a few moments, then he asks again, 'Grandfather, do I have a voice?'
   You answer involuntarily, 'Yes.'
   He repeats the question. You look at him and nod 'yes', making him understand. The child falls silent again. Then he asks, 'So why am I alive?'

He buries his face under your clothes. As if he wants to put an ear to your chest to listen for some sound from within. He hears nothing and shuts his eyes. Inside himself everything must make a sound. If only you could enter inside him and tell him the story of Baba Kharkash . . .

Your wife's unsteady voice reaches your ears:
   'Once upon a time there was a man named Baba Kharkash . . .'

You find yourself standing on the large branch of a jujube tree, stark naked. You've climbed up it to shake down jujubes for Yassin. At the base of the tree, Yassin is gathering the fruit. Without being able to help it, you start to urinate. Crying, Yassin moves away from the bottom of the tree and sits at the base of another. He empties the apples out of your scarf and replaces them with his jujubes, then ties up the bundle again. Digging into the ground with his small hands, he finds a door near the surface, secured with a big padlock. He opens the lock with a jujube stone and crawls underground.

'Yassin, where are you going? Wait! I'm coming down!'

Yassin doesn't hear your shouts and the door shuts behind him. You try to climb down from the tree, but the tree grows bigger and taller. You fall from the tree, but you don't hit the ground . . .

Your eyes are half-open. Your heart pounds in your ribcage. Yassin's head is still calmly buried under your clothes. Mirza Qadir is having a conversation with the guard beside the wooden hut. You try to open your eyes as wide as possible. You don't want to doze off again. You don't want to dream. But the heaviness of your eyes has crushed your will . . .

A woman's voice rings in your ears.

'Yassin! Yassin! Yassin!'

It's the voice of Zaynab, Yassin's mother. Her laughter echoes around your head. Her voice comes from somewhere far below. You step to the door that leads underground. It is closed. You call out for Zaynab but your voice reverberates on the other side of the door. Then the door opens and you see Fateh, the guard. He laughs and says, 'Welcome. Come in. I was waiting for you.'

You walk down into the ground. Fateh closes the door on you from the outside. From the other side of the door, the sound of his laughter rings in your ears.

'You've been wanting desperately to leave,' he says to you. 'Since the morning you've been driving me mad. So, go on!'

Underground it's cold and damp. You take in the smell of clay. There's a large garden, an empty garden, without flowers or vegetation, a garden with narrow paths covered in mud and lined with bare oak trees.

Zaynab sits naked under a tree, next to a little girl. You call out to her. Your voice doesn't seem to reach her. She lifts the little girl from the ground, wraps her in the apple-blossom scarf, kisses her on the cheek, then carries her away. Yassin is naked in a jujube tree. He says that the little girl is his sister, that he gave his mother his grandmother's apple-blossom scarf, the one you knotted into a bundle, so that she could put it around his sister because it's cold. But Yassin doesn't have a sister! A few days ago, Zaynab was only four months pregnant. How quickly she's given birth! How quickly her daughter has grown!

Yassin is shivering with cold. He wants to climb down from the tree, but he can't. The tree keeps growing bigger and taller. Yassin weeps.

You feel snowflakes land on your skin. The garden paths fill with snow.

Zaynab runs from one tree to the next. You call out to her again. She doesn't hear. She runs across the snow naked, the little girl in her arms. She laughs. Her feet leave no prints in the snow, but the sound of her steps echoes through the garden.

Yassin calls for his mother. His voice has become high-pitched like hers . . . You look at his body. It's the body of a young girl. In place of his small penis, there is a girl's vulva. You are overcome with panic. Without thinking, you call for Murad. Your voice is stuck in your throat. It reverberates in your chest. Your voice has become Yassin's – weak, confused, questioning:

'Murad. Murad! Murad?'

Someone grips your shoulders from behind. You turn around in horror. Mirza Qadir, smiling his habitual smile, says, 'Instead of the brains of our kids, Zohak's snakes are eating their pricks.'

Terror seizes you. You want to free your shoulders from Mirza Qadir's grip. But you don't have the strength.

You open your eyes. Your body is covered in sweat. Your hands tremble.

In front of you are two kind eyes:

'Father, get up. Your lift is here.'

Lift? For what? Where do you want to go? Where are you?

'Father, a vehicle headed to the mine.'

You recognize Mirza Qadir's voice and come back to your senses. Yassin sleeps quietly in your arms. You want to wake him.

Mirza Qadir says, 'Father, leave your grandson here. First, go there on your own, speak to your son in private. Then come back here. There's no room for both of you to spend the night at the mine. If your son sees his own child in this state, it'll be even worse . . .'

It's a good suggestion. Imagine what will happen when Yassin sees his father. He'll throw himself into his arms and, before you are able to say anything, he'll start shouting, 'Uncle's dead, Mummy's gone . . . Qader's dead, Grandma's dead! Grandfather cries . . .'

Murad's heart will stop when he hears Yassin. How could you make Yassin understand that he shouldn't say anything?

You accept Mirza Qadir's offer, but a sense of foreboding settles within you. How can you abandon your grandson, the only son of your only son, to someone you don't know? You've known Mirza Qadir for no more than two hours. What will Murad say?

'Old man, are you coming or not?'

It's the guard's voice. You remain silently where you are with Mirza Qadir, your eyes full of questions. What should you do? Yassin or Murad? Dastaguir, this is not the time for questions. Surrender Yassin to God and go to Murad.

'Old man, your lift's leaving.'

'I leave Yassin to you and God.'

Mirza Qadir's look and smile quell all your doubts and fears.

You take your bundle and head for the hut. A big truck awaits you. You greet the driver and climb in. The guard, who's standing in front of the hut – slouched, dusty, drowsy, dressed in a makeshift uniform, with the same half-smoked cigarette between his lips – lifts the wooden beam blocking the road and waves the driver through.

The driver exchanges a few words with you. The guard yells angrily, 'Shahmard! Are you going or not?'

Shahmard raises his hand in a gesture of apology and drives off.

The truck speeds onto the property of the mine. Through the rearview mirror, you watch the guard beside his hut disappear in a cloud of dust. You don't know why but his disappearance pleases you. Come on, the guard isn't a bad man. He's grief-stricken, that's all. You bless his father's soul. May he excuse you if you've thought ill of his son.

Your heart pounds in anticipation of visiting Murad. Your reunion is close now. This very road will take you to your son. Blessed be this road, a road that Murad has travelled many times. Would Shahmard stop the truck, so you could step down and prostrate yourself on this earth, before these stones, before these brambles that have kissed your son's feet? Blessed be the prints left by your feet, Murad!

'Did you wait long?'

Shahmard's question prevents you from kissing Murad's footprints.

'Since nine this morning.'

You both fall silent again.

Shahmard is a young man – about thirty years old, maybe even younger. But the blackened, smoked skin covering his bones and the lines and wrinkles on his face make him look older. An old astrakhan cap sits on his dirty hair. A black moustache covers his upper lip and yellow teeth. His head is pushed forward. His eyes, circled by black rings, dart about.

A partially-smoked cigarette rests behind his right ear. Its scent fills your nostrils. You imagine it is the smell of coal, the smell of the mine, the smell of Murad – the sight of whom at any moment now will light up your eyes. You'll kiss his forehead. No, you'll kiss his feet. You'll kiss his eyes and his hands like a child reunited with his father. Yes, you will be Murad's son. He'll take you into his arms and console you. With his manly hands he'll hold your trembling ones and say, 'Dastaguir, my child!'

If only you were his son – his Yassin. Deaf like Yassin. You'd see Murad but you wouldn't hear him. You wouldn't hear him say, 'Why have you come?'

'Have you come to work in the mine?' Shahmard asks.

'No, I have come to see my son.'

Your eyes drift over the rolling hills of the valley. You take a deep breath and continue.

'I come to drive a dagger into my son's heart.'

Shahmard gives you a confused look, laughs and says, 'Dear God, I'm giving a ride to a swordsman.'

With your gaze still lost in the valley, in its black stones, its dust and its scrub, you say, 'No, brother, it's that I bear great sorrow and sorrow sometimes turns into a sword.'

'You sound like Mirza Qadir.'

'You know Mirza Qadir?'

'Who doesn't know him? In a way, he's a guide for us all.'

'He's a man with a great heart. I didn't know him, but I just spent two hours in his company. I was won over. What he says is right. He understands sorrow. From his first glance, he instills trust. You can tell him whatever lies in your heart . . . In our day, men like Mirza Qadir are rare. Where is he from? Why is he here?'

33

Shahmard takes the half-smoked cigarette from behind his ear, puts it between his dry lips and lights it. He inhales deeply and says, 'Mirza Qadir is from the Shorbazar district of Kabul. He has only had a shop here for a short time. He doesn't like to talk about himself. He says little to those he doesn't trust. It took me a year to find out where he came from and what brought him here.'

Shahmard falls silent again. But you want to know more about Mirza Qadir, the man to whom you've entrusted your grandson. Finally he continues:

'He had a shop in Shorbazar. In the daytime

he'd work as a merchant and, in the evenings, as a storyteller. Each night a crowd would gather at the shop. He was a popular man who commanded great respect. One day his young son was called up to serve in the army. A year later he returned. He'd been made an officer and trained in Russia. This didn't please Mirza Qadir. He didn't want his son to have a military career. But the son liked the uniform, the money and the guns. He ran away. Mirza disowned him. The sorrow killed his wife. Mirza left Kabul. His home and shop remained behind. He came to the coal mine, where he worked for two years. With his first savings he set up that shop. From morning to evening he sits there, writing or reading. He's beholden to no one. If he likes you, he'll respect you, but if he doesn't like you, best not to let even your dog pass his shop . . . Some nights I stay with him till dawn. The whole night he reads stories and poems. He knows the *Book of Kings* by heart . . .'

Mirza Qadir's words ring in your tired ears. He spoke about Rostam and Sohrab, and of the Sohrabs of our day . . . The Sohrabs of today don't die, they kill.

You think about Murad. Your Murad isn't a Sohrab who would kill his own father. But you . . .

You are a Rostam. You'll go and drive the dagger of grief into your son's heart.

No, you don't want to be Rostam. You're

Dastaguir, an unknown father, not a hero burdened with regret. Murad's your son, not a martyred hero. Let Rostam rest in his bed of words; let Sohrab lie in his shroud of paper. Return to your Murad, to the moment when you will hold his black hands in your trembling hands and your wet eyes will meet his exhausted eyes. When you will have to seek strength from Ali, asking for help in saying what you must say:

'Murad, your mother gave her life for you . . .'
No, why begin with his mother?
'Murad, your brother . . .'
No, why his brother?
But then with whom should you begin?
'Murad, my child, the house has been destroyed . . .'
'How?'
'Bombs . . .'
'Was anyone hurt?'
Silence.
'Where's Yassin?'
'He's alive.'
'Where's Zaynab?'
'Zaynab? . . . Zaynab's . . . in the village.'
'And mother?'
Then you should say, 'Your mother gave her life for you . . .'

And Murad will start to weep.

'My son, be strong! These things happen to all men one day or another . . . If she was your mother, she was also my wife. She's gone.

When Death comes, it makes no difference whether it is for a mother or a wife . . . My son, Death came to our village . . .'

And then tell him about his wife, tell him about his brother . . . And then tell him that Yassin's alive, and that you have left him with Mirza Qadir because he was tired. He was sleeping . . . Don't say anything about his condition.

The noise of a truck coming from the opposite direction disrupts your conversation with Murad. It passes at high speed, raising clouds of dust. Dust erases the lines of the valley. Shahmard brakes.

'Will you spend the night with your son?' he asks.

'I don't know if there will be a place for me.'

'He'll find something.'

'Anyway, I have to get back. I left my grandson with Mirza Qadir.'

'Why didn't you take him with you?'

'I was afraid.'

'Of what?'

'Why should I upset you with all this, brother.'

'Don't worry about that. Tell me.'

'Alright, I'll tell you.'

Shahmard stays silent. As if he doesn't want to goad you. Maybe he thinks you don't want to talk. How could you not? When the village was destroyed, with whom could you sit and weep? With whom could you share your grief? With whom could you mourn? Everyone mourned their own dead. Your brother sat next to a pile of rubble, listening hopefully for a familiar voice to rise from beneath collapsed roofs and walls. Your maternal cousin, weeping, picked through the rubble for a piece of clothing or a scarf to use as a burial shroud. Your brother-in-law, lying next to a dead cow in the demolished barn, laughed as he suckled milk from its stiffened udder . . .

But you had Yassin. He couldn't hear your sobs, but he could see your grief. With whom did *you* sit? Whom did *you* comfort? You wanted to run from everybody. You were like an owl perched high on a ruin, or in an abandoned cemetery. If it weren't for Murad, if it weren't for Yassin, you would never have left that place. Thank God for Murad, for Yassin. You'd have stayed amid ruins till you turned to dust . . .

Dastaguir, where have you wandered off to this time? Shahmard wants you to explain why you didn't bring Yassin and you have drifted off into daydreams. Say something to him. Tell him about your people. Make an effort. They deserve some prayers. Who so far, apart from Mirza Qadir, has offered you their condolences? Who has prayed for the deliverance of their souls? Allow others to say the Fatiha prayer for your dead and to share your suffering. Say something!

And you speak. Speak of the ruins of your

village, of your wife, your son, your two daughters-in-law, Yassin . . . And weep.

Shahmard is mute. His eyes dart, restlessly seeking appropriate words. He finds them. He whispers the Fatiha. He offers you his condolences and falls into silence again.
    You continue. You speak of Murad. Of how to tell him about the death of his mother, his wife and his brother. Still Shahmard remains silent. What should he say? All of his rage at hearing your story has gone to his legs. His feet are heavy. You can tell from the speed of the truck.
    You also fall silent.

The bouncing of the truck and the drone of the engine make you feel sick. You want to close your eyes for a while.
    A military jeep appears behind the truck. It overtakes you, throwing up dark dust.

Within a black billow of dust, you see Murad's wife running naked in front of the truck. Her damp hair streams behind her, parting the dust – as if she were sweeping away the dust with her hair. Her white breasts dance on her chest. Drops of water fall from her skin like dewdrops.
    'Zaynab! Get out of the way of the truck!' you shout to her.
    Your voice is confined to the truck. It doesn't reach outside. It reverberates endlessly around the cab. You want to roll down the window and free your voice so it can reach Zaynab. But you don't have the strength. You feel heavy. Your

bundle weighs on your knees. You want to lift it up and put it beside you. But you don't have the strength. You untie it. Inside the apples have become black, they've turned to coal . . . Coal-apples. You laugh to yourself. A bitter laugh. You want to ask Shahmard about the mystery of the coal-apples. In place of Shahmard, Murad sits at the wheel. You can't prevent yourself from crying out. You don't know if it's from fear, surprise or joy.

Murad doesn't look at you. He stares at the road, at Zaynab. You shout his name again. Still Murad doesn't hear. It's as if he too has gone deaf.

Zaynab continues to run in front of the truck. The dust gradually settles on her white, damp skin. A veil of black dust covers her body. She is no longer naked . . .

The jolts of the truck blur your view of Zaynab. She and the road disappear in a cloud of dark dust.

You take a deep breath and glance furtively towards the driver's seat. Murad isn't there. Thank God. You've woken up. You look around silently. Your bundle is at your side. An apple has rolled out on to the seat.

Nervously you look in front of the truck again. Zaynab is not there. Zaynab threw her naked body headlong into the fire. She was burned alive. She was burned naked. She left this world naked. She burned to death before your very

eyes . . . How will you tell all this to Murad? Do
you have to? No. Zaynab is simply dead. Like
everyone else. There's nothing more to it. She
died like all the others – in the house, beneath
the bombs. She is bound for Paradise. We are
the ones burning in the fires of Hell. The dead
are more fortunate than the living.

What fine words you've learned, Dastaguir.
But you know they're of no use. Murad's not
the sort to ponder matters or withdraw calmly
to a corner and cry. Murad is a man. He is
Murad, son of Dastaguir. He's a mountain of
fortitude, a vast land of pride. The smallest
slight to his honour and he catches fire. Then
he either burns himself or causes others to
burn. The death of his own mother, wife and
brother won't go unanswered. He'll seek vengeance. He has to take revenge . . .

On whom? What could he do alone? They'll
kill him, too. Dastaguir, have you lost your
mind!

All you have left is a son, and you want to
sacrifice him? Why? To bring back your wife
and your other son? Swallow your anger. Leave
Murad alone. Allow him to live. Let my tongue
be still! Let my mouth fill with dust! Murad,
sleep in peace.

After exploring your pockets, you pull out your
box of naswar and offer some to Shahmard. You
put a small amount into the palm of his hand
and place some on your own palm before
putting it under your tongue.

Silence.

You watch the rocks and scrub race past. It's not you who are passing them. No. It's as if they are passing you. You're not moving. It's the world that's moving. You've been condemned to exist and watch the world pass, to watch your wife pass, to watch your children pass . . .

Your hands tremble. Your heart flutters. Your sight goes dim. You roll down the window of the truck to refresh yourself. The air isn't refreshing. It has become thick, heavy and black. It's not your sight that has gone dim, it's the air that has grown dark.

'Dastaguir, what have you done with my scarf?'

It's Murad's mother. You see your wife at the base of the hills, running at the same pace as the truck. You untie the bundle and let the coal-apples fall out. Then you let the scarf blow out of the window. The cloth dances through the air. Murad's mother runs after it, dancing as she goes.

'We've arrived.'

The image of Murad's mother reflected in the pools of your pupils is lost to the ripples of Shahmard's voice.

You open your wet eyes. The truck is nearing the mine. You sense that Murad is close. Your chest tightens, your heart swells, your veins constrict, your blood freezes . . . Your tongue has become a piece of wood, a charred piece, half-burned, an ember, a silent piece of coal . . . Your throat is dry. Water! You swallow your naswar. The smell of ash fills your nostrils. You take a deep breath. You smell Murad. You fill your lungs to their utmost with his scent. For the first time, you realize how small your lungs are and how big your heart is – as big as your sorrow ...

Shahmard slows the truck and turns to the left. He comes to a halt at the entrance to the mine. A guard appears from a wooden hut, just like the one at the start of the road. He asks for papers from Shahmard, looks over them and begins a conversation. You sit silently. You don't move a muscle. Actually, you wouldn't have the strength to do so if you wanted to. You hold your breath. For a few moments, you're nothing but a hollow shell. Your lifeless gaze falls through the grille of the mine's large iron gate. You sense that Murad is waiting for you beyond the gate. Murad, don't ask Dastaguir why he has come.

The truck passes through the gate and enters the grounds of the mine. At the foot of a large hill lies a line of concrete workers' quarters. Which of them is Murad's? Men with blackened faces, wearing metal construction helmets, come down the hill as others climb up. You don't see Murad among them. The truck heads towards the small concrete buildings and stops in front of one. Shamard suggests you get out and ask the mine's foreman about your son.

You experience a moment of confusion and don't react. There isn't enough strength in your hand to open the door. You are like a child who

doesn't want to be separated from his father.
You ask Shahmard, 'Is my son here?'

'Of course, but you'll have to ask the foreman
where.'

'Where is the foreman?'

Shamard points out a building to the right of
the truck.

Your weak, trembling hand has difficulty
opening the truck door. You put your feet on
the ground. Your legs are of no use. They don't
have the strength to hold you up. But your body
is not heavy. It's the heaviness of the air that's
pressing down on your body. The air is weighty
and thick. You rest your hand on your waist.
Shahmard passes your bundle through the window and says, 'Father, I'm heading back to town
between five and six. If you want to come, wait
for me at the gate.'

Bless you. You say this to yourself. To him
you only nod. Your tongue doesn't have the
strength to move. Words, like the air, have
become heavy . . . The truck moves off. You
remain nailed to the ground in a cloud of dust.
A few black-faced miners walk by. Murad? No,
Murad's not among them. Come on, go to the
foreman and ask.

You try to move. Your legs are still tired and
weak. It's as if they are sunk into the depths of
the earth, all the way down to its molten centre
. . . Your feet burn inside your shoes. Wait a
while. Take a deep breath. Calm down. Move
your legs. You can walk. So walk.

You reach the foreman's building and stop outside the door. It's an imposing door. Like the entrance to a fortress. What might be on the other side? Probably a mineshaft. One that is long and deep, that goes right down to the depths of the earth, all the way down to furnaces of molten rock . . .

You place your hand on the doorknob. It is burning hot.

Dastaguir, what are you doing? Are you going to plunge a dagger into the chest of Murad, your only remaining child? Can't you keep your troubles to yourself? Leave Murad alone! One day he'll find out. It's better if he hears it from someone else's lips.

What should you do then? Go and disappear from his life? No! What, then? You can't tell him today, you're exhausted, turn back! You'll come back tomorrow. Tomorrow? But tomorrow it'll be the same story, the same anguish. Knock on this door then! Your hands have become heavy. You step back.

Where are you going, Dastaguir? Can't you decide? Don't abandon Murad. Take the hand of your son like a father and teach him about life.

You walk up to the door. You knock. The door creaks loudly. The shaven head of a young man peers out. He is blind in his right eye. A fine web of red blood vessels worms over the white of the eye. With a gesture of his head he asks you what you want. Gathering your resolve, you say, 'Salaam. Murad, the son of Dastaguir, is my child. I have come to see him.'

The man opens the door wider. The inquiring expression has left his face. Taken aback, he turns his head to a man who sits writing at a large desk at the far end of the room.

'Foreman sir, Murad's father is here.'

On hearing these words, the foreman freezes. His pen drops on to his desk. His eyes bore into yours. A weighty silence fills the space between you. With all your strength, you draw yourself up and enter the room. But the silence and the strange expression of the foreman gradually burden your shoulders. Your legs tremble. Your body begins to stoop again. Dastaguir, what have you done? You have asked for Murad. You are going to kill Murad . . . No, may all be well. You won't speak to him. If he asks you why you've come, you'll say something else, an excuse. You'll say that his uncle visited the village, and you returned together by car to Pul-i-Khumri. Taking advantage of the opportunity, you came to the mine to get news of Murad. That's all. Afterwards you're returning to the village . . . Stay well, Murad!

The foreman stands and limps towards you. He places his heavy hand on your tired shoulder. It's as if the mine, with its big hill, its coal and its square cement buildings, rests there on your shoulders. Your body stoops even further. The foreman circles around you. He's very tall. It's his left leg that makes him limp. He is a mountain next to you. His mouth is open. As if he's about to devour you. His big black teeth are concealed under a dirty moustache. He smells of coal.

'Welcome, brother. You must be tired. Sit down.'

He directs you towards the wooden chair in front of his desk and then limps back to his place on the other side of the table. You sit down, keeping your bundle pressed against you. On the wall in front of you, just above the foreman's chair, hangs a large framed portrait of him. He wears a military uniform and, under his black moustache, a victorious smile.

The foreman, sitting in his chair again, starts to speak, slowly and carefully.

'Murad is down the mine. It's his shift now. Would you like tea?'

In a quavering voice, you reply, 'God protect you, sir.'

The foreman calls to the man who led you inside and sends him for two cups of tea.

You are relieved that Murad isn't available right away. It'll give you some time to come up with coherent answers and words of comfort. Maybe the foreman can help you. You ask, 'When will he be off work?'

'At about eight this evening.'

Eight this evening? Shahmard will be returning at six. Where will you go till eight? What will you do? Could you spend the night here? And what about Yassin?

'Good brother, Murad is fine. He has received news of the incident that has stricken his family. May God absolve them and give their souls peace . . .'

You don't hear the rest of the foreman's words. Murad has received news? You repeat the words to yourself a few times. As if you don't understand what they mean. Or you didn't hear correctly. After all, at your age one grows hard of hearing and misunderstands.

You ask loudly, 'He has received news?'

'Yes, brother, he knows.'

Then why didn't he return to the village? No, it can't be your Murad. It must be another Murad. After all, your son's not the only one with that name. In this very mine there are probably ten men with his name. The foreman hasn't understood that you're looking for Murad, son of Dastaguir. He must also be hard of hearing. Start again.

'I'm talking about Murad, son of Dastaguir, from Abqul.'

'That's right, brother, I'm referring to him, too.'

'My child Murad learned that his mother, his wife and his brother have died and he . . .'

'Yes, brother. He even heard about you, that you . . . May God protect you.'

'No, I'm alive. His own son's alive too . . .'

'Praise God . . . '

Why praise God? If only Yassin and Dastaguir had died as well! That way a father wouldn't have had to witness the frailty of his son, and a son the helplessness of his father. What has become of Murad? Something must have happened to him. The mine has collapsed and he has been entombed in coal. Swear to God, foreman, tell the truth. What has happened to Murad?

Your eyes flit about. They seek an answer from every object: from the worm-eaten table; from the portrait in which the foreman is immortalized; from the pen lying lifelessly on the paper; from the ground that trembles under your feet; from the roof that is collapsing; from the window that will never be opened again; from the hill that has devoured your child; from the coal that has blackened his bones . . .

'What has happened to Murad?' you ask in a loud voice.
    'Nothing, thank God, he's fine.'
    'Then why didn't he come to the village?'
    'I didn't allow him to.'
    The bundle of apples falls from your knees to the ground. Once more, your eyes search the room before fixing on the dirty lines of the foreman's face. Once more, your mind fills with questions – and with hate.
    Who does this foreman think he is? What does he take himself to be? You're Murad's father. Who is he? He has taken Murad from you. There is no longer any Murad. Your Murad's gone . . .

The foreman's gruff voice echoes around the room:

'He would have gone. But I didn't let him.
Had I, he would have been killed as well . . .'

What of it? Death would have been better than
dishonour!

The servant brings two cups of tea and gives one
to you and the other to the foreman. They begin
a conversation. You can't hear what they're
saying.
  With trembling hands you hold the cup on
your knees. But your legs are trembling too. A
few drops of tea spill on to your knees. They
don't burn you. No, they do burn you, but you
don't feel it. You're already burning within.
Within, a fire burns that is more fierce than the
tea. A fire stoked by the questions of friends and
enemies, relatives and strangers:
  'What happened?'
  'Did you see Murad?'
  'Did you speak to him?
  'What did you tell him?'
  'What did he do?
  'What did he say?'

And how will you answer them? With silence.
You saw your son. Your son has heard about
everything. But he didn't come for his dead
mother, wife and brother. Murad has lost all his
integrity, he has become shameless . . .

Your hands tremble. You put the cup on the
table. You know that your sorrow has taken
shape now. It has become a bomb. It will

explode and it will destroy you too – like Fateh the guard. Mirza Qadir does indeed know all about sorrow. Your chest collapses like an old house, an empty house . . . Murad has vacated his place inside you. What does it matter if an abandoned house collapses?

'Your tea will get cold, brother.'
    'It's not important.'

The foreman continues:
    'Until two days ago Murad wasn't doing well. He wouldn't go near bread or water. He withdrew to a corner of his room. He didn't move. He didn't sleep. One night he went out of his quarters completely naked. He joined the group of miners who spend the night beating their chests in repentance around a fire. At dawn he began to run around and around the fire and then he threw himself into the flames. His companions came to his aid and pulled him out . . .'

Slowly you open your clenched fists. Your shoulders, drawn up to your ears, relax. You know Murad. Murad isn't one to remain calm. He either burns or causes others to burn. He either destroys or is destroyed. He didn't set fire to others this time, he burned himself. He didn't cause destruction, he was destroyed . . . But why didn't he come back and burn together with his mother's corpse? If Murad were Dastaguir's Murad, he would have returned to the village, he would have beaten his chest beside his lost ones, not around a fire . . . They told him that you too were dead. The day when you do die – and you will die, you won't live eternally – what will he do? Will he see you have a proper burial? Will he lower your coffin into a grave? No, without shroud or coffin your body will fester under the sun . . . This Murad isn't your Murad. Murad has sacrificed his soul to the rocks, the fire, the coal, to this man sitting before you, whose hot breath stinks of soot.

'Murad is our best worker,' the foreman says. 'Next week we'll be sending him on a literacy course. He'll learn to read and write. One day he'll hold an important post. We're sending him because he's a model mine worker who earns respect for being an enlightened, hard-working youth who's committed to the revolution . . .'

You don't hear the rest of the foreman's words. You think of Mirza Qadir. Like him you must choose whether to stay or leave. If you see Murad now, what will you say to him?
'Salaam.'
'Salaam.'
'You've heard?'
'I've heard.'
'My condolences.'
'Condolences to you too.'
And after that? Nothing.
'Goodbye.'
'Bye.'
No, you have nothing else to share with each other. Not a word, not a tear, not a sigh.

You pick up the bundle resting on your knees. You no longer want to give it to Murad. The apple-blossom scarf smells of your wife. You stand and say to the foreman, 'I am going. Please tell Murad that his father came, that he's alive, that Yassin, his son, is alive. With your permission . . .'

Goodbye Murad. Head bowed, you walk out of the room. The air has grown thicker, heavier and darker. You glance at the hilltop. It seems bigger and blacker . . . The men coming down the hillside have faces that are even more tired and even more black. You don't want to look at these faces, the way you did when you first arrived at the mine. What if Murad were among them?

You head towards the gate of the mine. You have only taken a few steps when a shout stops you:

'Father!'

The voice is unfamiliar, thank God. You recognize the foreman's servant hurrying stealthily to your side.

'Father! What I say stays between us. They told Murad that it was the mujahiddeen and the rebels who killed his family . . . in retaliation for his working here at the mine. They terrified him. Murad doesn't know you're alive.'

You are now even more hopeless and forlorn. You glance back at the foreman's building and grab the servant by the arm.

'Take me to my child!'

'It's not possible, father! Your son is working at the bottom of the mine. If the foreman knew, he'd kill me. Go, father! I'll tell him that you came.'

The servant wants you to release him. Confused, you place your bundle on the ground. You explore your pockets. You take out your box of naswar, hand it to the servant and request that he give it to Murad. He grabs the box and rushes away.

Murad will recognize your box of naswar. After all, he gave it to you himself, the first time he was paid. As soon as he sees the box, he'll know you're alive. If he comes after you, you'll know Murad is your Murad. If he doesn't, you will have no Murad anymore. Go, get Yassin and return to the village. Wait there a few days.

You quicken your step towards the exit of the mine. You reach the gate. Without waiting for Shahmard, you walk towards the hills. A sob constricts your throat. You close your eyes and weep quietly within. Dastaguir, be strong! A man doesn't weep. Why not?! Let your heart's sorrow overflow!

You wind around the side of the first hill. You want naswar. You have none. Maybe the box of naswar is already in Murad's hands.

You slow your pace. You stop. You bend down. You take a pinch of grey earth between your fingertips and place it under your tongue. Then

you continue on ... Your hands are clasped
behind your back, holding tightly the bundle
you tied from the apple-blossom scarf.

54